Dear Matilda
Best Fishes
Melody
the Mermaid x

A Mermaid's Melody

Written by Rach
Illustrated by Trac

For Oliver and Eliot and their vivid imaginations.
You are everything that is beautiful to me.

Where watery stars glisten, as waves lap against the sand,
And crash against the rock pools, defining sea from land,
A mermaid heard cries of an oyster, abandoned by the sea,
Imprisoned by a rock pool, desperate to be set free.

Mermaid spoke, "How did you come to get here,
so very far from home?"

"Entwined in fishing net, I escaped amongst the dense sea foam...
Before reaching open waters, I was captured by the tide...
Please rescue me fair maiden," the tiny creature cried.

In his plight, poor frightened Oyster, had not noticed the maiden's tail.
Adorned from waist to tail fin with pearlescent fishy scales,
Hair glistening in the sunlight, as blue as the Azure Sea,
A voice to enchant and enrapture, a Merrymaid was she.

Tiny Oyster gazed in amazement, as he could not believe his eyes,
As legends of the Merfolk, he'd thought, were nothing more than lies,
But no longer could Oyster deny these tales,
as sat on rocks as plain as could be,

Was a mystical Mermaid creature, sent by Neptune to set him free.

Mermaid spoke of a world of wonder, her world beyond the beach,
In the depths of the deepest oceans where mere mortals cannot reach.

Here is the birthplace of mermaids, so mystical and fair,

"I shall take you there, on a crest of a wave, to live without a care."

I shall take you there, on the crest of

In the depths of the deepest oceans where

By now the sun was rising and the tide was getting low,
Said Oyster, "If you help me escape this tidal pool,
such kindness I'll bestow....
My shell conceals a secret, hidden from mortal view...,
Forged from a grain of sand, a gem I'll surely make for you."

With that he opened wide his shell, to the Mermaid's great delight,
And reflected in the tidal pool, rippled a radiant lustrous light.
For nestled deep within the centre of Oyster's plain and simple shell,
Lay a single pearl, so beautiful, t'was the treasure of which he did tell.

Captivated by the pearl, the Mermaid sang a melody.
The gentle sea became the song, the lapping waves the harmony.
Mesmeric and enchanting, her chorus cast a Mermaid spell,
A verse to rouse the waves, to release this poor sea shell...

As she sang, each haunting word appeared to float upon the breeze,
Each note still ringing in the air, until lost upon the seas.
Spellbound by the lyricism of the Mermaid's rhyming verse,
Poor Oyster did not notice that the waves were getting worse.

Suddenly, from calm waters, the tide began to swell and heave,
"Prepare yourself, my Oyster friend, the time has come to leave....
For Neptune, in his majesty, has heard my Mermaid's incantation."
(Along with every mollusc, seahorse, starfish and crustacean!)

Neptune summoned his great storm council, in the depths far off the shore,
To speak in ancient tongue, a ritual written in Merfolklore,
Gathered in the caverns, the Sea-Morgans raised their mighty hands,
Their tridents poised, a tumultuous wave was sent back t'ward the land.

Mermaid smiling, she picked up Oyster, and held him tightly in her hand
As in the distance, she could see cascading waves approaching land.
Reassuringly, she pulled Oyster close, and whispered gently in his ear,
"I'll keep you safe, my little friend, close your eyes and do not fear."

The waves had grown in magnitude as they continued on their course,
And reaching shore they hit the rocks, with overwhelming force,

Waves swept them up and tossed them in a tumbling swirling motion,

Until finally,

with one large SPLOSH, they dropped back beneath the ocean.

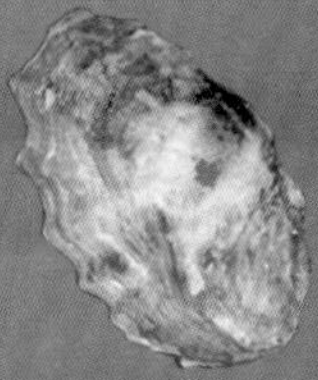

Mermaid and her seafolk friends,
had freed Oyster from his plight,
And once in calmer waters Oyster spoke with great delight,
"As promised you have returned me, to dwell on the ocean floor,

From now on, Mermaids and Oysters will be friends forevermore."

As a simple gift of friendship, Oyster grows his beloved pearls,
To adorn the shimmery skin of all the pretty fish-tailed girls.
"A single pearl I'll fashion, from the smallest grain of sand,
To symbolise when Mermaid rescued Oyster from the land."

Our Special thanks to

Bill, for his sustaining love and
strength to carry me along life's journey.

David for his unfaltering support
and never ending patience.

And finally to Tracy for her creative vision in
transforming a collection of words
into a visual delight.